Jasmine

*Jasmine, from Anne Pumpkin's photograph.*

# Jasmine

written and illustrated by

## Roger Duvoisin

Alfred A. Knopf: New York

*Library of Congress Cataloging in Publication Data*

Duvoisin, Roger Antoine, 1904- .   Jasmine.

*Summary:* When Jasmine the cow begins wearing a hat, the other barnyard animals criticize her for trying to be different.

I. Title.   PZ7.D957J25   [E]   74-39597   ISBN: 0-394-82444-X   ISBN: 0-394-92444-4 (Lib. bdg.)

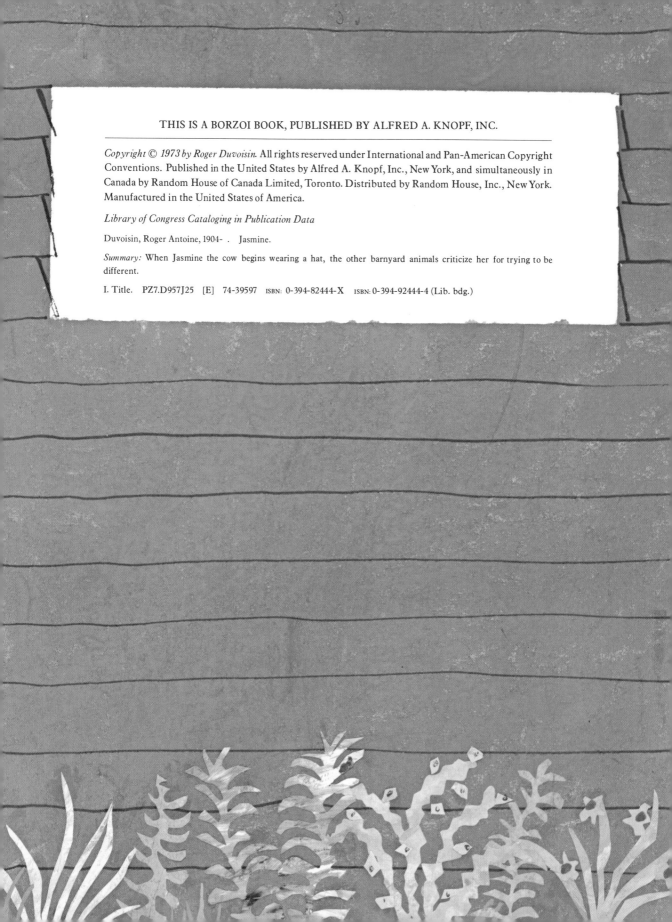

"What's this I see lying in the middle of the barnyard?" wondered Jasmine. "It looks like a sick bird with long fuzzy feathers. Perhaps it's dead."

She walked up to it and pushed it gently with her left horn. The horn went through it. It sat so tightly on her head that she could not shake it off. So she thought, "I had better go down to the pond to look at myself in the water and see what is on my head."

It was not a dead bird. It was a feathered hat, the kind great-grand-mothers wore when they were young. Jasmine was so pleased with the hat that she could not tire of looking at her reflection.

She finally said, "This hat is just right for me. I will wear it. I don't see why a cow can not wear a fancy hat as ladies do."

How Jasmine's friends laughed when she returned to the barnyard! "Jasmine," they asked, "didn't you see what fell on your head?"

"It did not fall on my head. I put it there. And it's going to stay there. Such a lovely hat."

"Jasmine, have you lost your mind? How foolish you look!"

Jasmine only smiled. "I know what *I* like and what's good for me. You can say what you want. I could not care less."

"Jasmine, please," said Rose the sheep, "you wouldn't want NOT to be like all of us."

"You can be as you like," said Jasmine, "that's very well with me. And I will be as I like. Each one to her own taste."

From then on Jasmine proudly went around the farm with her hat. She wore it every day to the pond to admire her reflection in the water. She even slept in it.

When the farmers, Mr. and Mrs. Pumpkin, and their granddaughter Anne saw Jasmine with the hat they laughed. Mrs. Pumpkin said, "Isn't she dainty? Look at the nice way she tosses her head to one side to put the hat in place. How did she find this hat?"

"It's probably one of those many old family hats which are gathering dust in the barn attic," said Mr. Pumpkin.

"Please," said Anne, "let her keep it. She is so lovely with it."

The animals kept looking at hatted Jasmine with unfriendly eyes.

Clover the cow said, "I do not like a cow who wants to be different. It's a good-for-nothing cow if you ask me."

"She thinks she is better than we," said Canary the cow.

"Pretentious," said Ida the hen. "That's what she is."

"Or sick," added Rose the sheep.

So they went on. But Jasmine kept her hat on and loved it.

"Good for her," said Cotton the cat sitting quietly with his tail curved around his paws. "As I always say, live and let live. This takes pluck and Jasmine has it."

"You know," put in Straw the horse, "in the old days horses wore straw hats to keep cool in summer — hats with holes for their ears."

"Maybe it's not so silly to wear a hat after all," said Pig. "Of course, I wouldn't wear one myself."

"I wouldn't either," cried the whole barnyard together.

But Noisy the dog said, "Jasmine's hat comes from the attic up in the barn. There are enough hats there for all of you. I can go and fetch them. That is, if you want to look like Jasmine."

For the rest of the day they talked about the hats in the attic.

Clover asked, "Canary, would *I* look prettier with a hat?"

"That's what I was wondering about myself," answered Canary.

"Ida," said King the rooster to his favorite hen, "you can wear a hat if you wish. I myself wouldn't wear one for it would hide my fine comb and I would no longer look like a rooster."

The next day Noisy piled up the attic hats in the barnyard.

Every beast and bird ran to pick a hat. The barnyard was full of dancing animals with great-grandmother and great-grandfather hats and caps, old doll and baby hats.

Anne clapped her hands with joy when she saw the joyous animals.

"They all want to be like our dainty Jasmine!" she laughed.

It was a happy hat day.

That night while she rested in the meadow, Jasmine thought many thoughts about the happenings of the day. In the morning she walked up to the barn with a smile. She took off her hat and hid it behind the old cider press.

It was Donkey who first noticed that Jasmine was not wearing her hat. He nudged Rose the sheep saying, "Hey, look at Jasmine. No hat today. What is she up to now?"

Rose gave such a jerk of surprise that her plumed hat nearly fell off. "There she goes again," she snapped, "not wanting to be like everybody."

The news that Jasmine was hatless spread quickly. Soon everybody was talking about it.

Clover, in her flowered hat, shook her head and said, "See, I was right. Cows who want to be different are good-for-nothing cows."

"And see how silly she looks with her bare head," said Canary.

"Pretentious," said Ida the hen. "I knew it all along."

"Or, I repeat, SICK," added Rose the sheep.

"And she may be even sicker if she has a sun stroke," said Pig, trying to see Jasmine through the lace trimming of her own bonnet.

Thus day after day they talked, for every morning they saw Jasmine hatless, browsing in the meadow just relishing the good grass.

It was most annoying.

Petunia the goose was the first to say what they all began to feel. "I must admit that my hat begins to be heavy on my head. I wonder, aren't we all more handsome without a hat?"

"I woundn't be seen without a hat," said Mother pig.

"Neither would I," said Piglet, Donkey, Clover, Canary and Straw.

"I rather agree," said Jenny the mare. "On the other hand, maybe Jasmine isn't so stupid to go bareheaded."

And, behold, without a word all the birds and beasts swarmed up to the barnyard to shake off their caps, hats and bonnets. Soon everything was back in the attic.

Now, what did they see the next morning? Why, they saw Jasmine with her hat on, admiring her reflection at the edge of the pond.

The sight made them so angry that they gathered in the meadow to decide what should be done about Jasmine.

"I told you she was a no-good cow," said Clover. "Now it's time to put an end to her mischief!"

"We must order her to take off that silly hat," shouted Canary.

"Right!" cried Rose. "And if she refuses, let's pull it off."

"Yes, let's! We must not permit her to make trouble for us here," cried all the animals.

All that is, except Petunia and Cotton the cat.

"I don't see why cows or anybody else can't dress as they please," said Petunia.

"I don't either," said Cotton licking his paw.

The two followed the crowd to the pond where Jasmine loved to graze. Clover, Canary, Rose and Ida led the parade with their heads low and their eyes dark with anger. The horses swished their tails right and left while the pigs twisted and untwisted theirs. The goat kept her horns low, ready to pounce. King strutted on, followed by his hens. And they all sang, "Off with Jasmine's hat! Off with Jasmine's hat! Jasmine's hat into the pond!"

As the noisy parade arrived at the pond to surround Jasmine, the singing and the shouting suddenly melted into silence. Jasmine, wearing her hat, was smiling at a camera which Anne was ready to click. Mr. and Mrs. Pumpkin were there, too.

When she saw the parade Anne said, "Oh, I will take a picture of Jasmine with all these animals around her. She will be the queen of the barnyard!"

Anne and her camera changed anger into fun. After all, if Anne said so, Jasmine *must* be lovely with her hat. So, Clover and Canary stood on each side of Jasmine. Petunia, Rose and Cotton sat in front. King perched on Clover's head, and the other animals crowed close, not to be left out of the picture.

"Now, SMILE!" Anne cried.

They all smiled.

*"Click,"* went the camera.

Then, still smiling, all the animals trotted back to the barnyard. And this is how Jasmine became the beloved queen of the Pumpkin farm. Jasmine who did not mind *NOT* being like everyone else.

*About the Author*

Roger Duvoisin needs little in the way of introduction. He has written and illustrated some forty books for children and is the illustrator of more than one hundred others. Some of the titles in his popular Veronica and Petunia Series (Knopf) are now available as Pinwheel paperbacks. Roger Duvoisin is a past winner and runner-up for the Caldecott Medal.